Charlene Loves to Make Noise

Charlene Loves to Make Noise

by Barbara Bottner

Illustrated by Alexander Stadler

RUNNING PRESS
PHILADELPHIA · LONDON

9   8   7   6   5   4   3   2   1
Digit on the right indicates the number of this printing

Library of Congress Cataloging-in-Publication Number 2002100456

ISBN 0-7624-1297-6

Designed by Frances J. Soo Ping Chow
Acquired by Patty Aitken Smith
Edited by Patty Aitken Smith and Susan K. Hom
Typography: Modern Mt Wide

This book may be ordered by mail from the publisher.
Please include $2.50 for postage and handling.
But try your bookstore first!

Running Press Book Publishers
125 South Twenty-second Street
Philadelphia, Pennsylvania 19103-4399

Visit us on the web!
www.runningpress.com

To my husband G.K., whose shyness
brings out the best of me

—B. B.

For Iyana

—A. S.

When she wakes up in the morning,
Charlene listens to the birds and wind chimes.

Charlene knows which food to feed her trigger fish.

Charlene likes to have one place in her room that is neat.

Charlene likes little dogs
and BIG people.

Charlene watches everybody and notices everything.

Charlene likes it better when her best friend
walks into the classroom first.

Charlene speaks quietly or not at all.
Charlene is a very good listener.

Charlene thinks she wants to raise her hand,
but she's not sure if she knows the right answer.

"Say Abe Lincoln," she whispers to her friend.

"You do it!"

"I can't!" she whispers again.

They are both quiet.

If you tell Charlene a secret, it will be safe forever.

Charlene has a lot to say, but not always with words.

Charlene likes to daydream. Then, she wonders
what she missed but is too afraid to ask.

Charlene loves parties,
as long as they are for someone else.

She makes a birthday present only she could think of.

Charlene writes her best friend a poem.

But she does not want her to read it out loud.

Or show it to anyone.

Charlene laughs hard when something is really funny.

Then she hopes nobody saw.

Charlene does frog imitations.

But only if you ask her.

When her friends clap for her,

Charlene gets embarrassed—and goes home.

When Charlene is alone, she plays the drums.

Charlene loves to make noise!

At the end of the day,

Charlene promises herself not to be shy.

Tomorrow.

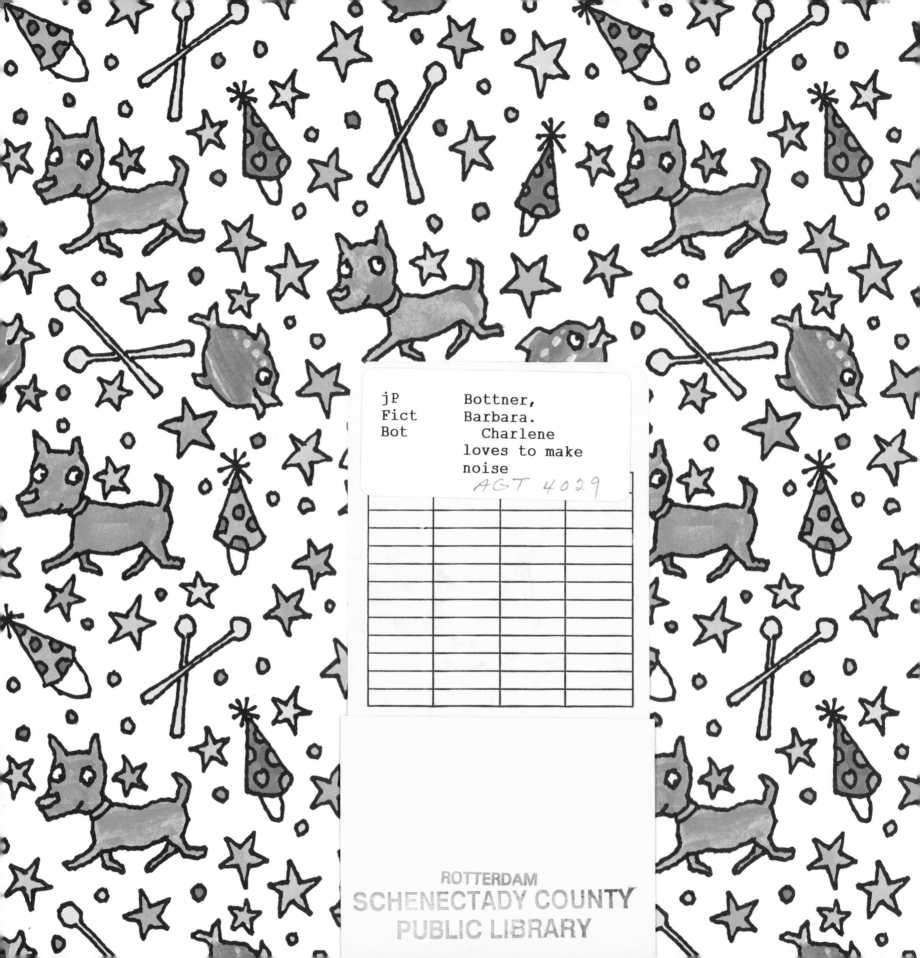